For Amber and Florence,
And for Emmi Cat

First edition 2015

Library of Congress Catalog Card Number 2013957388
ISBN 978-0-7636-6912-6

15 16 17 18 19 20 CCP 10 9 8 7 6 5 4 3 2 1

Printed in Shenzhen, Guangdong, China

This book was typeset in Aunt Mildred.
The illustrations were done in pencil and watercolor, combined digitally.

Candlewick Press
99 Dover Street
Somerville, Massachusetts 02144

visit us at www.candlewick.com

How to Catch a MOUSE

Philippa Leathers

CANDLEWICK PRESS

This is Clemmie.

Clemmie is a brave, fearsome mouse catcher.

She is excellent at stalking and chasing.

She is patient and alert.

She knows everything about
how to catch a mouse.

In fact, Clemmie is such a fearsome mouse catcher
that she has never even seen a mouse.
All the mice are afraid of me, thinks Clemmie.

But Clemmie is always
on the lookout.

What's that?

A mouse has a long pink tail . . .

but this is not a mouse.

There are no mice in *this* house!

What's that?

A mouse has two round ears . . .

but this is not a mouse.

There are no mice in *this* house!

What's that?

A mouse has a whiskery, pointy nose . . .

but this is not a mouse.

There are no mice in *this* house!

What a good mouse scarer I am,
Clemmie thinks.
There are no mice in this house.
And she curls up for a nap.

But wait. . . .

Crinkle!
Rustle!
Bang!

What's that?

It has a long pink tail.

It has two round ears.

It has a whiskery, pointy nose.

It's a mouse!

Clemmie has finally seen a mouse,
but it got away.

But Clemmie has learned a new trick that
might just help her catch that mouse. . . .

Meow!